BOOKS BY MAIL

Produced by Kroha Associates, Inc.
Middletown, Connecticut.

Printed in the United States of America.

ISBN 1-56326-118-9

Look On
The Bright Side

One day toward the end of summer, Minnie and her friends were sitting on Minnie's porch trying to think of something to do.

"It's too hot to ride bikes or walk to the park," Daisy said, "and I'm tired of playing in the sprinkler."

"It seems like we've done everything a jillion times," Penny added.

"I know," Minnie said as she petted Fifi. "Let's go to the movies!"

"That's a great idea!" Daisy exclaimed. "It will be cool in the movie theater."

"And we can get a big tub of popcorn to share," Clarabelle said.

"And my favorite movie is playing!" Penny added.

"Do we have enough money for tickets?" asked Daisy, looking in her purse. "I've only got fifty cents."

Minnie ran into her house and came back with her pink and white, polka-dotted piggy bank. She turned it upside down and shook it, but only two dimes fell out.

"I found a dollar in my pocket," Penny exclaimed.

"Well, I don't have any money at all," Clarabelle sighed. "I used my whole week's allowance to buy new hair bows. I guess we're not going to the movies today, after all."

"Let's look on the bright side," Minnie said, smiling. "We may not have enough money to go to the movies right now, but we can use the money we have to help us earn some more!"

"How?" asked Daisy.

"Well," Minnie explained, "we can build a lemonade stand. I have some sugar, and we can use this money to buy some lemons to make lemonade. Then we'll sell the lemonade and make the money we need to go to the movies. It's so hot today, we'll have lots of customers."

"That's a great idea, Minnie," her friends agreed.

They hurried to the corner store and bought some large, juicy yellow lemons. Minnie counted out the money very carefully.

"Look," she grinned when she was done paying. "We even have a lucky nickel left over!"

When they got back to Minnie's house, everyone helped make the lemonade.

Minnie and Penny squeezed the lemons. Daisy and Clarabelle added sugar and water. Everyone tasted it to make sure it was just right.

"Now let's make our lemonade stand," Minnie said. "I'll put the lemonade in the refrigerator. By the time we finish the stand, the lemonade will be nice and cold."

Minnie found some boxes and boards in her garage. Penny and Clarabelle helped carry them to the driveway. They set the boxes on end and laid the boards across the box tops to make a counter. Meanwhile, Daisy got a big sheet of paper and a felt-tipped pen and wrote a sign that read "Cold Lemonade 25¢."

Finally, the stand was finished.

"I'll put up the sign," Daisy said, picking up a roll of tape.

"I'll go get the lemonade," Clarabelle said. "Come help me carry the cups, Penny," she called as she ran toward the house.

"Wait up," Penny shouted after Clarabelle. "My shoelace is untied." But as Penny bent over to tie her shoelace, she bumped into Daisy. When she did, Daisy dropped the sign and knocked her elbow against the edge of the stand.

"Ow, ow, ow!" Daisy yelled. "I hit my funny bone — and it doesn't feel funny at all!" She hopped up and down, rubbing her elbow.

Minutes later, Daisy's elbow was still hurting. As Daisy hopped around rubbing her arm, Clarabelle came out of the house. But Daisy didn't see Clarabelle carrying the pitcher of lemonade, and hopped right into her. THUMP! Clarabelle fell down.

"Oh, no!" Penny cried as a river of lemonade trickled past her. Clarabelle and Daisy looked at each other.

"I'm sorry, Clarabelle," Daisy said, helping up her friend. "Are you okay?"

"Yes," Clarabelle said. "But I spilled the lemonade, and we're out of lemons!"

"And we've only got a nickel left, so we can't buy more, either," Penny added.

But Minnie wasn't ready to give up. "Look on the bright side," she said. "We still have sugar and ice. And there are lots of oranges in the fruit bowl in the kitchen. We'll sell orangeade instead!"

"Well, okay," the girls agreed. Daisy changed the sign while Minnie, Penny, and Clarabelle made the orangeade. When the orangeade was finished, they carried it outside very carefully. Then they sat down and waited for customers.

They waited a long time. Two boys rode by on their bikes, but they didn't stop. The city bus driver waved and honked as he drove past, but no one got off at the bus stop. Mrs. Magee walked past with her puppy, Casey. "Would you like some orangeade, Mrs. Magee?" Minnie called.

"Oh, no, thank you, Minnie," Mrs. Magee called back. She just waved and kept on walking.

"We might as well drink this orangeade ourselves," Penny said. "No one is going to buy a single glass. I don't see any customers anywhere."

"Wait, here comes one now!" Minnie exclaimed, pointing to a little girl who was running toward them. Just then, the little girl tripped and fell. She threw out her hands to catch herself, and her money rolled down the sidewalk. PLINK, PLUNK, PLONK, it fell through the grating over a storm drain.

"Are you hurt?" Minnie asked as she and the others ran to help the little girl.

"I'm okay," the girl cried. "But all my money fell through the grate!"

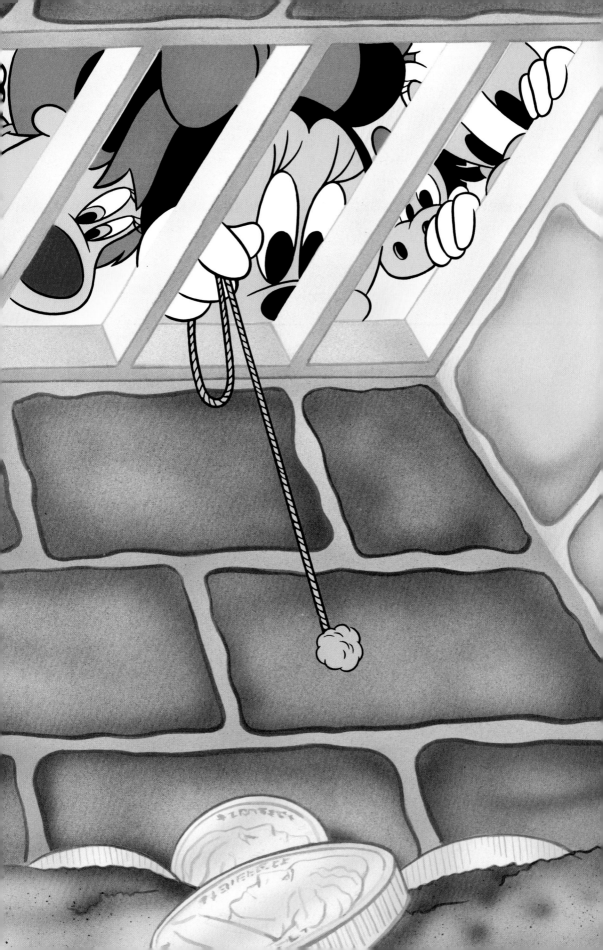

"Maybe we can fish it out," Minnie suggested. She took a piece of chewing gum from her pocket and chewed it for a minute. Then she tied the gum onto a piece of string. Next, she knelt and slowly lowered the string through the grate. Everyone watched anxiously as Minnie dangled the string over the coins, trying to stick them on the gum. But try as she might, Minnie couldn't fish the coins out.

"I wanted some orangeade, and now I can't buy any," the little girl said as she started to cry.

"Cheer up," Minnie said. "We'll give you all the orangeade you want for free!"

"Oh, thank you," the little girl said, smiling as Minnie handed her a cup. "It's so hot out, this will taste great!" Sipping slowly, she started walking home.

"I think I'll have some, too," Daisy said. "I'm really thirsty."

"Me, too," Clarabelle and Penny chimed in.

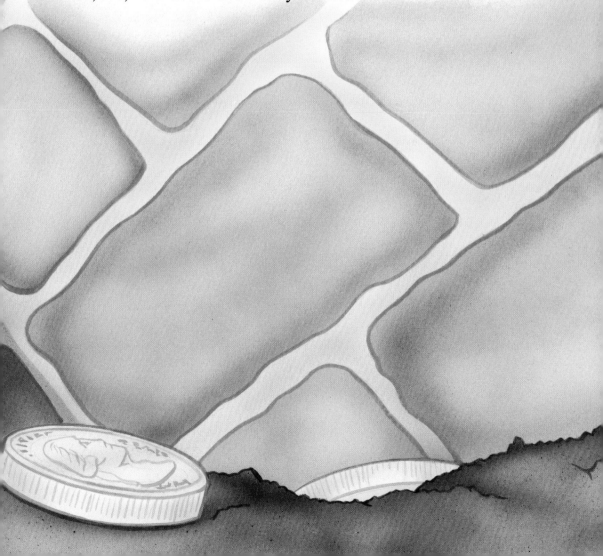

But before they could pour themselves any orangeade, a puppy bounded up the sidewalk, its leash trailing behind it. "Why, that's Mrs. Magee's puppy, Casey!" Minnie exclaimed. "She's probably looking for him! We'd better catch him and tie him up so he will be safe until Mrs. Magee gets here."

"Quick!" Penny yelled. She grabbed for the puppy's leash — and missed! Casey dodged the other way, barking playfully.

"Here puppy, puppy," Clarabelle called. But Casey wouldn't come.

"I know!" Daisy shouted. "Let's circle around him, so whichever way he goes, one of us will get him!" The girls ran around the puppy. But he was too fast for them! This time, he ran right between Clarabelle's feet.

Suddenly, Fifi came into the yard and saw the puppy. She ran after him, and when Casey headed for the lemonade stand, Fifi followed. The puppy ran under the stand — and so did Fifi! The stand wobbled. It shook. It tipped this way and that. Then — CRASH — over it went!

"Oh, no!" the girls shouted as they looked at what was left of the stand. The boxes were tipped over, the boards were scattered every which way, and Fifi and Casey were happily lapping up all the spilled orangeade.

Mrs. Magee came running up the walk. "You found Casey!" she exclaimed. "I was so worried about him! Thank you so much for keeping him until I got here! You all deserve a big reward!"

"Oh, that's okay," Minnie said. "We didn't want your puppy to get lost, Mrs. Magee. We don't expect a reward!"

"Well, I'm giving you one, anyway," Mrs. Magee said, smiling at them. "You certainly earned it!" She reached into her purse and handed Minnie some money.

"Thank you," Minnie and her friends said.

"Thank *you*, girls!" Mrs. Magee smiled and led Casey away.

Minnie looked down at the money in her hand and started to laugh. "Guess what!" she exclaimed. "We can go to the movies after all!"

Soon the girls had everything cleaned up and were on their way to the movies. After they bought their tickets, they went to the refreshment stand.

"Let's get the super-duper size popcorn," Clarabelle said.

But when Minnie counted out their money, they discovered that they had five cents less than they needed.

"That's too bad," Penny said. "That popcorn smells so good!"

"And I'm hungry," Clarabelle sighed. "If we had only five more cents!"

Then Minnie remembered something. She started to grin as she pulled out one shiny nickel from her pocket and plunked it on the counter.

"That's our lucky nickel!" Daisy shouted. "It's the one left over from buying the lemons!" Everyone started to laugh.

At last, everyone was sitting in the cool, dark theater waiting for the movie to start. "I guess you're right, Minnie," Daisy said as she passed her friend the popcorn tub. "It does pay to look on the bright side!"

That sure was a funny day! Luckily, everything worked out in the end. Looking on the bright side did the trick!